JACK'S MEGA MACHINES
THE DINOSAUR DIGGER

Alison Ritchie and Mike Byrne

SIMON & SCHUSTER
London New York Sydney Toronto New Delhi

At Mechanic Jack's magical Rally Road workshop a digger was in for repair.
Jack oiled the pistons and tightened the excavator arm.

THE DINOSAUR DIGGER

The loader bucket was crooked and some of the metal teeth were missing.

Jack fiddled and banged and bashed until the digger was as good as new.

"Righto, Riley, let's go!"

Riley jumped up onto the cab, ready for action. Every time Jack took a machine on a test drive, they had an amazing adventure.

Jack started the engine—

BBBBRRRUUUUM!

With a loud CLUNK the workshop doors flew open and the digger powered out into . . .

"Wow!" gasped Jack.

Strange flying creatures squawked and shrieked in the sky, and they could hear the roars of huge beasts.

Suddenly, the ground began to shake . . .

Before they knew it, a stampede of baby dinosaurs was on top of them.

Jack skilfully veered and swerved as they raced past.

He tipped this way and that, and reared up on the back wheels, balancing the digger on its bucket like an acrobat.

The baby dinosaurs disappeared in a cloud of dust, but right behind them was a massive Tyrannosaurus Rex!

It came charging along the path, gnashing its sharp teeth and thrashing its tail.

Just in time, Jack manoeuvred the digger out of the way.

"Phew, that was CLOSE!" said Jack. "But look, Riley!

He's chasing the babies. They'll be his dinner.

Quick! We've got to help them!"

The digger was perched dangerously on top of a mountain.

Jack could see the dinosaurs sprinting along towards a steaming swamp. There was only one thing to do – he would have to go straight down the mountainside!

Jack revved the powerful engine and swung the
digger over the edge of the slope.

It was so steep, he thought the digger might tip over
and somersault straight into the swamp below.

But the digger's enormous wheels gripped the ground and they reached the bottom safely. The baby dinosaurs were trying to scramble through the swamp before the T. rex got to them. But they were sinking fast! "What now, Riley?" said Jack.

Riley barked at a tall tree in the middle of the swamp. "Brilliant idea, Riley!"
Jack raised the excavator arm and grabbed the treetop in its sharp teeth.

Then he pulled the tree across the swamp and held it tight in the excavator jaws.

The baby dinosaurs scrabbled on to the tree trunk
and clambered out of the mud.

 The last little dinosaur was nearly out of danger when . . .

. . . the T. rex thundered to the swamp edge, roaring with anger!

As the last baby dinosaur
rushed across, Jack let go of
the treetop and

BOING!

The tree flipped back like a catapult and bashed the T. rex on its head. It fell over in a dizzy heap.

Suddenly Jack and Riley were surrounded by huge dinosaurs, and were lifted onto their backs like heroes! The parents were saying thank you for rescuing their babies.

"I don't think that T. rex will be bothering you again," said Jack.
The baby dinosaurs cheered loudly.

Soon it was time to get back to Rally Road.

"WOW! This digger is the BEST!" said Jack,
when they got back to the workshop.

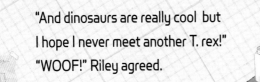

"And dinosaurs are really cool but
I hope I never meet another T. rex!"
"WOOF!" Riley agreed.

For Jonny

– AR

For Rose

– MB

SIMON & SCHUSTER

First published in Great Britain in 2013.

This special edition published in 2021 by Simon & Schuster Uk Ltd

1st Floor, 222 Gray's Inn Road, London, WC1X 8HB

Text copyright © 2013 Alison Ritchi

Illustrations copyright © 2013 Mike Byrne

Paper engineering by Maggie Bateson

Concept © Simon & Schuster Uk Ltd

The right of Alison Ritchie and Mike Byrne to be identified as the author and illustrator of this work
has been asserted by them in accordance with the Copyright, Designs and Patents Act, 1988

A CIP catalogue record for this book is available from the British Library upon reques

ISBN: 978-1-4711-4426-4

Printed in China

10 9 8 7 6 5 4 3 2 1

**Look out for more of
Jack's amazing adventures
in a bookshop near you!**

**Jack's Mega Machines:
Rocket Racing Car**

**Jack's Mega Machines:
Supersonic Submarine**

**Jack's Mega Machines:
Mighty Monster Truck**